JOANNE B. HACKMAN

FOUL PLAY
AND OTHER PUZZLES
OF ALL KINDS

IVAN MORRIS

Foul Play and Other Puzzles of All Kinds

Illustrations by
HUGH CASSON

VINTAGE BOOKS
A DIVISION OF RANDOM HOUSE
NEW YORK

FIRST VINTAGE BOOKS EDITION, MAY 1974
Copyright © 1972 by Ivan Morris
Illustrations copyright © 1972 by Sir Hugh Casson

All rights reserved under International and Pan-American Copyright Conventions. Published in the United States by Random House, Inc., New York. Originally published in Great Britain by The Bodley Head, Ltd., in 1972.

Library of Congress Cataloging in Publication Data

Morris, Ivan I
  Foul play and other puzzles.

  1. Puzzles. I. Title.
GV1493.M58 1974   793.7'3   73-17186
ISBN 0-394-71050-9
        Manufactured in the United States of America

CONTENTS

*For the meaning of *, **, and *** see Preface*

Preface   9
1 The Flying Chinaman *   15
2 Profitable Memories ***   16
3 Farmer Jones and his Trees *   17
4 Law and Honour **   18
5 Decimalization **   20
6 Old Woman **   21
7 Two Charades * and **   22
8 The Lump of Gold *   24
9 Adam and Eve *   25
10 A Curious Irish Verse ***   26
11 International Law *   27
12 Chances **   28
13 The Green Coat ***   29
14 The Maze *   31
15 Squares **   31
16 Big Ben **   32
17 Gaston's Execution *   33
18 Sleeping Tablets *   34
19 The Accident *   36
20 The Busker ***   38

21	No Incest **	39
22	Two Japanese Statesmen *	40
23	Modern Transformations * and ** and ***	41
24	Castling into Mate ***	42
25	The Word-Lover **	43
26	Bees **	44
27	Remarriage *	45
28	The Massacre **	46
29	Riddle *	46
30	Lovers' Chat **	47
31	A Simple Word Game **	48
32	Professor Honda's Children *	48
33	The Egyptian Army ***	49
34	Odd Verb Out *	50
35	Hijacker *	50
36	Outside the Hut *	52
37	Aboard Japan Airlines **	54
38	ABCD ... WXYZ **	56
39	Blackbirds *	57
40	Scrambled Letters **	57
41	King Olav *	58
42	Professor Baba's Last Request ***	60
43	The Canny Landlord *	62
44	Charles XII's Interrupted Game ***	64

45 Prunella and her Lover * 67
46 Professor Baba's Little Game *** 68
47 Hippies ** 70
48 Belinda's Lovers * 73
49 Digits * 74
50 Mrs Tabako's Balls ** 74
51 American Scholars * 76
52 Lord Dunsany's Problem ** 78
53 Japanese Uncles ** 79
54 Tempus Fugit ** 79
55 Ship of Fools ** 80
56 Foul Play * 82

PREFACE

The creation and solution of puzzles must surely rank among the more ludicrous pastimes of *homo sapiens*. 'As if that lot didn't have enough unsolved problems already', one can imagine the pyramid-shaped observer from Mars saying to his companion, 'they have to go and invent useless ones about blind Japanese professors in mazes and men being each other's uncles. These people *deserve* to be unhappy.' And yet.... Perhaps it is precisely because we are surrounded by so many actual insolubles that we (or at least the puzzlers among us) choose to spend time with these artificial tormentors. As one amateur has well expressed it: 'In a world full of important puzzles whose answers are ambiguous, inconclusive, and often non-existent [one can enjoy] testing [one's] wits on these gratuitous ones, which have definite (and rather unimportant) solutions.'

Many puzzle-lovers are no doubt running away from the 'real problems of life', but compared to some of the more fashionable escapes the invention and resolution of number games and riddles and logical posers seem innocuous enough. These psychological implications were called to my attention a few winters ago in New York when I went to get an inoculation against the current strain of influenza—a precaution which, needless to say, promptly caused the illness that it was meant to prevent. After injecting me with his noxious fluid the doctor (a general practitioner whom I was visiting for the first time) asked me whether I suffered from anything except the fear of catching the 'flu. 'Yes indeed,' I replied, 'I have chronic insomnia.' 'And what do you do when you can't sleep?' he asked. 'I try solving puzzles,' I replied, 'and sometimes I make up my own.' 'Ah hah!' said the doctor. 'And hasn't it ever occurred to you *why* you do that?' Strangely enough, it never had occurred to me (I'd always assumed that I did puzzles because they were 'fun') but now the morbid implications of my pastime were suddenly revealed. Why did I prefer balancing 324 fat ladies on a seesaw to weighing the living difficulties that encompassed me? Obviously it was high time that I consulted someone who dealt with matters of this sort, and the influenza doctor was fortunately able to suggest the name of a specialist (an old friend of his). But shortly afterwards I misplaced the piece of paper on which he had written it and thus missed an opportunity to get at the truth.

Several years have gone by and through all the intervening vicissitudes I have remained a devoted puzzler. Strangely enough (considering that the square root of half my age is still less than five) experience has not made me any better at grappling with the mystifications of words, numbers, and ideas. If anything, I find them harder than I did in the past, and rarely do I achieve a rapid breakthrough, even with two-star puzzles. This in no way diminishes the pleasure of the chase, whose essence is the suspense, the anticipation, the act of struggling with a difficulty in the sure knowledge that a solution is at hand and that soon one will be released from the tension of ignorance.

As in my two previous collections I have added stars to each puzzle as follows: * for Brief Diversions, ** for Hard Nuts, and *** for Herculeans. I have often been called to task for either underrating or overrating the complexity of puzzles in my earlier books, and so I must repeat that these evaluations are quite subjective, being intended simply to give a rough idea of the relative difficulty so that experts need not be bored and beginners not discouraged.

Once again I extend my thanks to Sir Hugh Casson (incidentally a confirmed non-puzzler) for his drawings, which have transformed Professor Baba, Mr Tabako, Belinda, and the other *dramatis personae* of my puzzle world into living creatures whose existences, like ours, are beset with knotty problems, though usually of a rather different nature. My further gratitude goes to Dr Harry Hazard of Princeton for reading my manuscript in proof and making criticisms which were as valuable as they were acerbic, and to Mr Michael Knibbs for his further scrutiny. I also thank those friends and acquaintances who have furnished me with puzzles or ideas for puzzles; wherever possible, I have given due acknowledgement at the end of the respective questions.

A final word of thanks goes to my correspondents in different parts of the world (Tasmania, Singapore, Oslo, Pretoria, Bath, Florence, Bad Neuheim, and Pittsburgh, to name but a few of the places from which I have received letters) who have commented on my puzzles in the previous two books and often suggested alternative solutions which, though sometimes wrong, are far more ingenious than any I could have devised.

FOUL PLAY
AND OTHER PUZZLES
OF ALL KINDS

1
The Flying Chinaman

*

A Chinaman who weighs exactly one hundred pounds is being pursued by his enemies. He has been obliged to abandon all his wealth except for two solid gold balls, weighing ten pounds each, which he is carrying as he runs. Approaching a long, uneven, winding bridge that crosses a deep ravine, he is dismayed to see a notice that says (in Chinese) MAXIMUM WEIGHT ON THIS BRIDGE: 115 POUNDS. The bridge is the only possible way across the ravine, and his enemies are rapidly closing in on him. How does he get across the ravine safely with his two gold balls?

2
Profitable Memories
* * *

Each blank space in the following passage must be filled with words having the numbers of letters indicated. Each word must use all the letters in the preceding word plus one new letter, and the letters can be freely jumbled (e.g. O . . . go . . . tog . . . goat . . .). The passage, though unusual, makes perfect sense.

'1 think 2 is significant' said the man in the black 3 as he performed the 4 'that when we 5 a person we 6 a 7 memory of him. There will be a 8 against 9 when the 10 of memory is recognized.'

3
Farmer Jones and his trees

*

Farmer Jones decides to plant three trees so that each tree is at exactly an equal distance from the other two. He does this by planting them at the three corners of an equilateral triangle. Later he decides to plant four trees so that each one is at an equal distance from each of the others. How does he manage?

4
Law and Honour
* *

Chorax, an aspiring lawyer, borrows a large sum of money from Phaedo, promising to repay him when he wins his first case in court. Many years pass, yet he never takes on any case and refuses to repay the debt on the grounds that he has never won a case. Finally Phaedo sues him for repayment and Chorax decides to conduct his own defence. On the appointed day both men appear in white robes and high spirits. Chorax is confident that, whatever the outcome, he will be free of his debt; Phaedo, on the contrary, believes that he is now bound to be paid. Why are the two men so optimistic, and which of them (if either) is correct?

5
Decimalization
* *

On 1st January 1971 Crucifer provided a 'simple ruse' for converting from the new decimal currency back into shillings and pence: 'Provided it's more than five and less than fifty take any decimal penny figure, double it, then carefully put an oblique stroke between the resulting two digits—and you'll instantly be back (give or take a penny or two) in the cosy old world of shillings and pence. Try it and see. It works.'

Does it? If so, why? Why must it be less than fifty and more than five?

6
Old Woman
* *

The --- old woman on --- bent
Put on her --- and away she went.
'Come, --- my son,' she was heard to say,
'Whom shall we --- upon today?'

The blank spaces should be filled with four-letter
words. The same four letters appear in all five words.

(*Given to me by Mrs Hans Bielenstein*)

7
Two Charades

*

(a) My first, portentous goddess, at her birth
  With countless stars illuminates the earth.
  My next is off like arrow from the bow,
  When *auri sacra fames* bids her 'Go!'
  All apparitions that can chill the soul
  Are found in thee, my horror-breathing whole.

* *

(b) *My First:* Hail, foster-mother of our human race,
  With ample brow and solemn, melting eye:
  Thy graciousness is lovelier than grace;
  Pure is the cup of thy benignity.

My Second: And when thy feeble offspring trembling stands,
  Thy care and love my second part supply—

> Caressing softer far than human hands,
> To soothe, to freshen and to beautify.

My Whole: Let him who can, explore my hidden cause;
> Let him my devious courses turn who can;
> Art is but weak to grapple Nature's laws—
> I wave rebellious on the brow of man!

(*From L. B. R. Briggs, Original Charades, New York 1891*)

8
The Lump of Gold
*

'I'll give you a lump of gold if you solve this puzzle,' Mr Tabako said to his son. 'The lump weighs two ounces plus half its weight. How heavy is it?' Master Tabako received the lump. What was his answer?

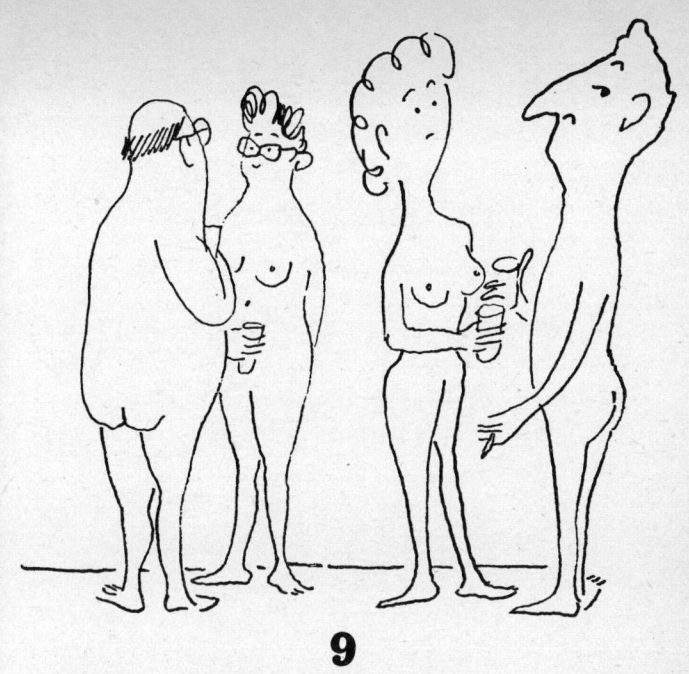

9

Adam and Eve

*

Arriving in Paradise, Bim found that everyone was stark naked. He carefully examined the company, but could recognize no one. Then, suddenly noticing a couple in the corner, he hurried over to them. 'Good evening, Adam and Eve,' he said. 'I have never met you, but I know who you are.'

How had Bim identified the couple (neither of whom was wearing a fig-leaf)?

10
A Curious Irish Verse
* * *

'Recently' writes James Michie, Esq., 'an old Irish manuscript of verses has fallen into my hands. The translation of one of them reads:

> 1 after women, that 2 3,
> And 4 maidens with 5 arts
> By 6 of moonlight, under 7 of trees;
> I, the King's 8, rue the 9.

What is so curious is that the nine blank spaces represent different anagrams, all comprising the same six letters.' Identify the missing words. (N.B. 3 is a proper name; there is an apostrophe in 5; 8 is an unusual word, but it appears in the Concise Oxford Dictionary.)

11
International Law

*

Air France flight 305 from Paris to Madrid crashes on the exact border between the two countries and the wreckage faces in a direction parallel to the border. Would unidentified survivors be buried in the country of destination (Spain) or in the country of departure (France), or does the nationality of the aeroplane's registration decide the matter?

12
Chances
* *

One of the fascinating things about the book entitled *Canada; Our Friendly Neighbour to the North* is that p. 36 and p. 278 each has precisely as many words with an odd number of letters (industrious, wholesome, etc.) as with an even number (sturdy, law-abiding, etc.)

(a) A glance at the first and last words on p. 36 shows that at least one of them has an odd number of letters. What are the chances that the other also has an odd number?
(b) The last word on p. 278 has an even number of letters. What are the chances that the first word is also even?

13
The Green Coat
* * *

The procedure for solving this poem (by James Michie, Esq.) is the same as in number 2, except that letters may be repeated.

> On 1 day, 2 alert 3 old 4
> In 5 was 6, wearing green.
> 7 sneered at his coat,
> But he 8, 'Please note
> That this 9 10 clean.'

(N.B. 5 is a proper name; 9 and 10 include apostrophes.)

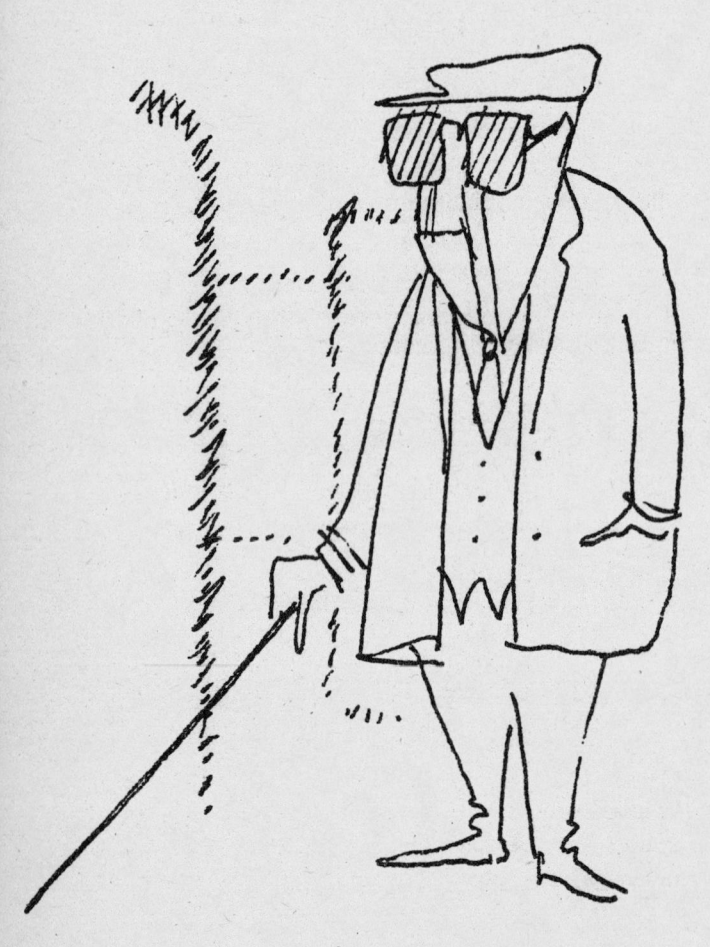

14
The Maze
*

Professor Fujita is visiting the Great Maze at Bishop's Tachbrook (Warwickshire), which has one entrance and one exit. Unfortunately the professor is completely blind and he cannot speak a word of English. How does he manage to get through the maze despite all the blind alleys and without any help from anyone?

15
Squares
* *

133,225 and 133,956 are the squares of two consecutive numbers. What is the square of the next consecutive number? (It is not necessary to take any square roots.)

16
Big Ben
* *

Professor Baba is visiting London. One day he is hurrying from the British Museum to Waterloo Station to catch the 10 o'clock train. In the distance he sees Big Ben and, while he is too far away to read the dial of the clock, he can tell that the two hands are together and from this he knows the precise time. What is it?

(Relayed by Master Wilson Kidde of Connecticut)

17
Gaston's Execution

*

Gaston, who is about to be executed, is allowed to make a final statement which must be either true or untrue. The executioner gives him a choice: if his statement is true, he will be guillotined; if it is false, he will be garrotted. After a few moments' thought Gaston utters a statement that makes it impossible to execute him. What does he say?

18
Sleeping Tablets
*

Mohammed A. Kruz is a chronic insomniac. His only effective medicine is the powerful barbiturate, Idiotal. Idiotal comes in two strengths, large and small, and Kruz keeps all the tablets in the same bottle. They are indistinguishable except by their size: the only way in which Kruz can tell whether a tablet is large is to compare it with a small one and vice versa.

When he arrived in Fez, Mr Kruz had exactly 100 tablets in his bottle, some large and some small, but he did not know how many were small and how many large. He decided to take a large tablet before retiring to bed. How many tablets may he have been obliged to extract at random from the bottle before being sure that he had found a large one?

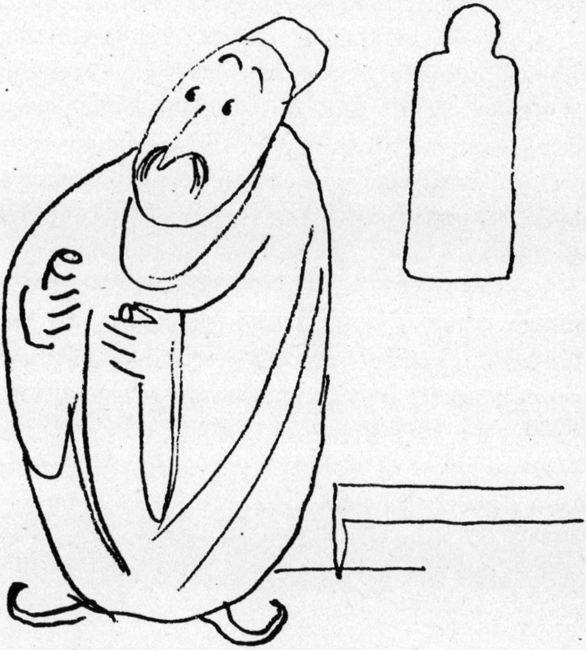

19
The Accident

*

James McKeetch and his son, Bruce, were speeding along the M1 Motorway one rainy night when suddenly their car skidded off the road. James was killed outright, but Bruce, though seriously injured, was still alive when the police arrived. He was rushed to Nottingham General Hospital and instantly wheeled into the emergency operating theatre.

'My God!' gasped the old surgeon on seeing Bruce's battered face. 'A rum coincidence if ever I saw one! This poor lad is my own son, Bruce. I cannot possibly perform the operation.'

How could the surgeon be correct about Bruce's identity? (N.B. Bruce has two parents and no stepparents.)

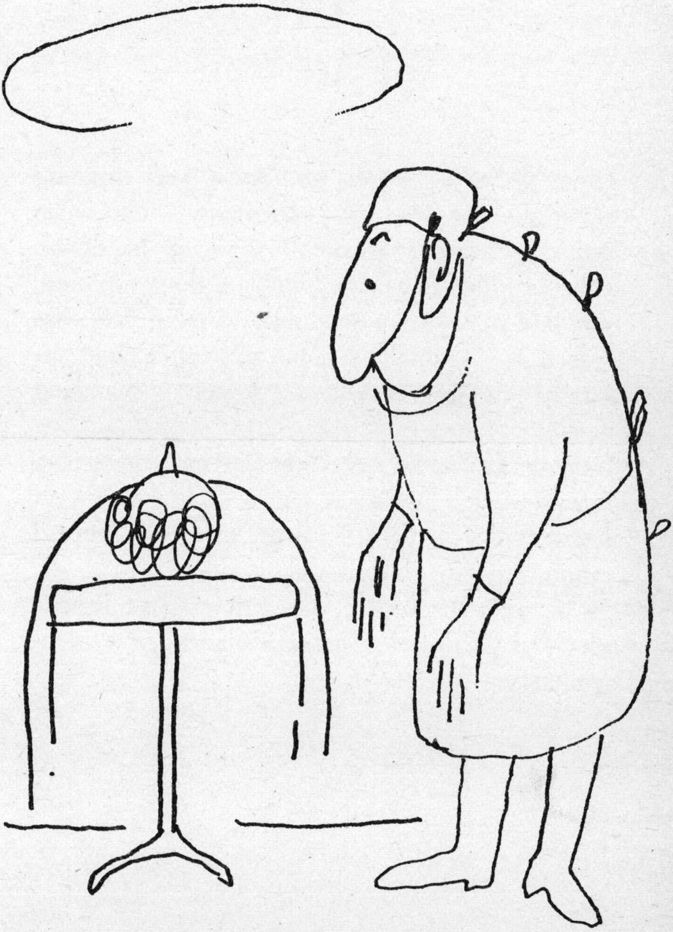

20
The Busker
* * *

The rules are the same as in number 2.
1 busker, who can 2 the same time 3 fire and 4 paper patterns without becoming 5 at the mixed images on his 6, will feel 7 on his almost 8 calm to sustain him when combining the roles of 9 and 10 artist.
(N.B. The 9th missing word is hyphenated.)

(Invented by Lady Violet Powell)

21
No Incest
* *

The following authentic epitaph dating from 1538 is quoted by H. V. Dudeney:

Two grandmothers with their two granddaughters;
Two husbands, with their two wives;
Two fathers, with their two daughters;
Two mothers, with their two sons;
Two maidens, with their two mothers;
Two sisters, with their two [half-]brothers;
Yet only six in all lie buried here;
All born legitimate, from incest clear.

How are these relationships possible?

22
Two Japanese Statesmen
*

Sugawara no Michizane, the great scholar-statesman and the deity of Japanese failures, was born in 845. When was he double the age of his main rival, Fujiwara no Tokihira, who was born on the same day in 871?

23
Modern Transformations

These modern transformations are done on the model of *cat* ... cot ... cog ... *dog*:

*

(a) *dove* into *hawk* in 5 steps,

*

(b) *money* into *power* in 6 steps,

* *

(c) *water* into *booze* in 10 steps,

* * *

(d) *blood* into *sweat* into *tears* in 8 and 10 steps respectively

(*All except b invented by Professor Herschel Webb*)

24
Castling into Mate
* * *

The following position occurred in an actual game between Emanuel Lasker and Sir George Thomas. Show how White can force a win in eight moves and enjoy the rare satisfaction of castling into checkmate.

[42]

25

The Word-Lover

* *

Philip, the main character in Christopher Hampton's play *The Philanthropist*, is a philologist and has an obsessive fascination with words. Towards the end, as the hopeless vacuity of his emotional life becomes apparent to him, he composes a brilliant anagram on I IMAGINE THE THEATRE AS REAL. The anagram expresses his loathing for the type of empty word-plays that have taken the place of authentic feelings in his life. What is it?

26
Bees
* *

The square root of half the number of bees in a swarm flew out upon a jessamine bush; one female bee flew about a male that was buzzing within the lotus flower into which he had been lured in the night; eight ninths of the whole swarm remained behind. How many bees were there?

(Invented by the great Hindu mathematician, Bhascara, ca. 1150 A.D.)

27
Remarriage

*

Is it possible according to canon law for a man to marry his widow's sister if she is totally unrelated to him by blood ties?

28
The Massacre
*

In the Great Massacre of Shimonoseki the Shogun's army killed 999,919 of the inhabitants, each of his soldiers killing an equal number, and each one killing more inhabitants than there were soldiers. How large was his army?

(*Based on an idea of Dudeney's*)

29
Riddle
*

What is the beginning of eternity,
The end of time and space,
The beginning of every end,
The end of every race?

30
Lovers' Chat
* *

The S.S. Olympia sails due east from Palos to Poros, then northwest to Tanos, and then due south to Nauplios. Belinda stands on the upper deck with her lover, Basil. 'Extraordinary!' he says. 'There are thousands of square miles of open sea, but at this moment we may be passing over the very same spot where we were a few days ago.' 'But surely,' says Belinda, 'the chances of our passing *exactly* over the same place are one in several thousand.' 'Not so,' says Basil. 'It is a hundred per cent certain to happen.'

If Palos lies west of the Tanos-Nauplios meridian, is Basil correct?

31
A Simple Word Game
* *

Take any three-letter combination (e.g. ONE) and add different letters in front of it to make as many words as possible (e.g. bone, cone, done, gone, hone, lone, none, pone, tone, zone = 10 words). The aim is to find a combination that will produce the largest number of words. My own record is thirteen. (No proper names allowed)

32
Professor Honda's Children
*

Professor Honda has four children. In 1972 their ages contained five figures of which all are odd, and they add up to fourteen. When were the children born?

(Based on an invention of Dudeney's)

33
The Egyptian Army
* * *

The rules are the same as in number 13; the 4th missing word is a proper name and the 12th is hyphenated:

1 like being 2 the Egyptian Army, though the pay is 3 on the 4. I sit well behind the 5 and 6 to the shells on the 7 ripping out 8 at 9, sending out 10 fellaheen to their 11 home. For me, war has a 12 attraction.

(*Invented by James Michie, Esq.*)

34
Odd Verb Out
*

Which verb does not belong in the list below, and why?
Bring, buy, catch, draw, fight, seek, teach, think.

(by Dr H. W. Hazard)

35
Hijacker
*

In November 1971 a hijacker on Northwest Airlines Flight 305 from Washington to Seattle demanded (and received) $200,000 in ransom cash and 'more than one parachute'. Subsequently he parachuted alone from the aeroplane in the middle of the night, carrying the money with him. What logical reason may he have had for demanding 'more than one' parachute?

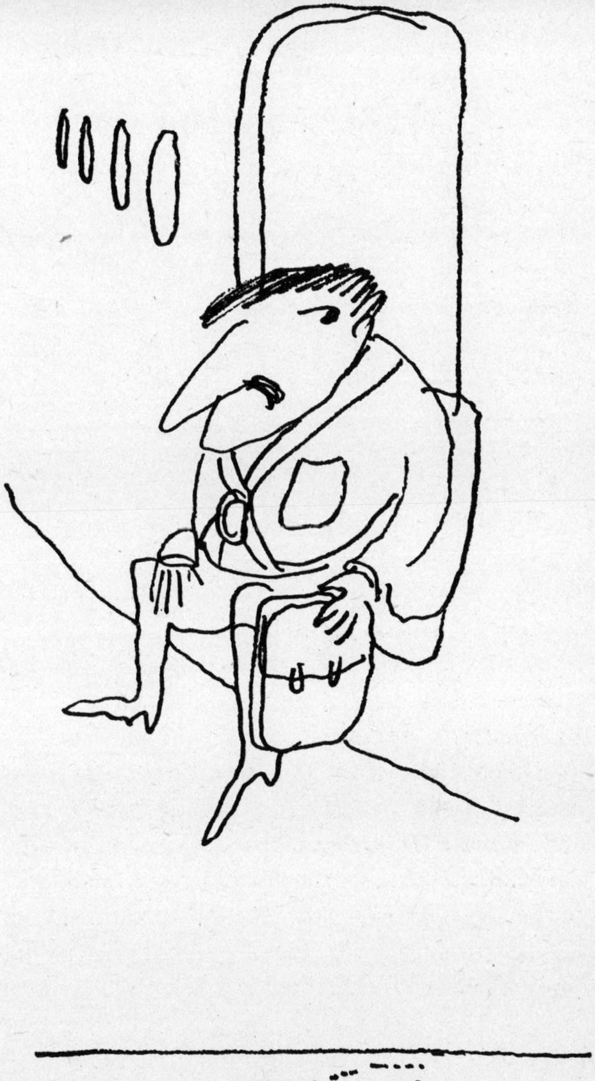

36
Outside the Hut

*

'Great Scot!' gasped Fingle as he left the hut. 'How can you stand this climate? What's the temperature now?'

'There's a thermometer there on the wall,' said Little Billy.
'Incredible!' exclaimed Fingle, looking at the thermometer. 'This can't be right. I never knew one could have such temperatures. Is this Fahrenheit or Centigrade?'
'As it happens,' replied Little Billy, 'it makes not the slightest difference.'
What is the exact temperature outside the hut?

37
Aboard Japan Airlines
** **

Watanabe, Tanabe, and Abe are the Captain, Assistant Captain, and Chief Stewardess aboard Japan Airlines Flight 500 to Honolulu, but not necessarily in that order. The passengers include Mr Abe, Mr Tanabe, and Mr Watanabe. Mr Abe lives in Tokyo. The Captain lives in Kamakura. Mr Tanabe has been a cripple since birth. The passenger whose name is the same as the Captain's lives in Yokohama. The Captain and one of the passengers, a well-known *sumō* wrestler, belong to the same Buddhist parish. Watanabe beats the Assistant Captain at *go*. Who is the Chief Stewardess?

(*Based on Dudeney and Gardner*)

Supplementary Mr Abe always carries a small bomb in his attache case when travelling by air. His aim is to protect himself because, as he believes, the chances that two passengers on the same aeroplane will be carrying bombs are far smaller than the chances that one passenger will be doing so. Is he correct in this belief?

38
ABCD...WXYZ
**

In Japan the great ninth-century religious leader, Kōbō Daishi, composed a beautiful Buddhist poem in which he used all forty-seven syllables in the *kana* syllabary once and only once. This has never been done in English and probably never can be. What is the shortest sentence you can compose which contains all the letters of the alphabet? (N.B. Initials, abbreviations, and roman numerals are not accepted.)

39
Blackbirds
*

Twice four and twenty blackbirds
Were sitting in the rain.
Jill shot and killed a seventh part.
How many did remain?

40
Scrambled Letters
* *

If you scramble all twenty-six letters in the English alphabet, you can produce trillions of combinations of letters. If you next take every possible group of twenty-five letters, scramble each group in turn, and add up all the resulting combinations, do you get a larger or smaller number than in the case of the twenty-six letter combinations? (N.B. It is not necessary to produce a single twenty-five or twenty-six letter combination in order to solve this.)

41
King Olav
*

Carefully read the following sentence once and once only. Nothing should be written down; everything should be done in your head.

The ferryboat *King Olav* leaves Trondheim with fifty passengers. It takes on double that number at the next port, and one third of the passengers disembark when the boat stops again. At the next port the square root of the number of remaining passengers disembarks, and ten more passengers get aboard when the boat reaches its following port of call. An hour later the *King Olav* reaches Oslo, its final destination.

How many times has the *King Olav* stopped on the way since leaving Trondheim?

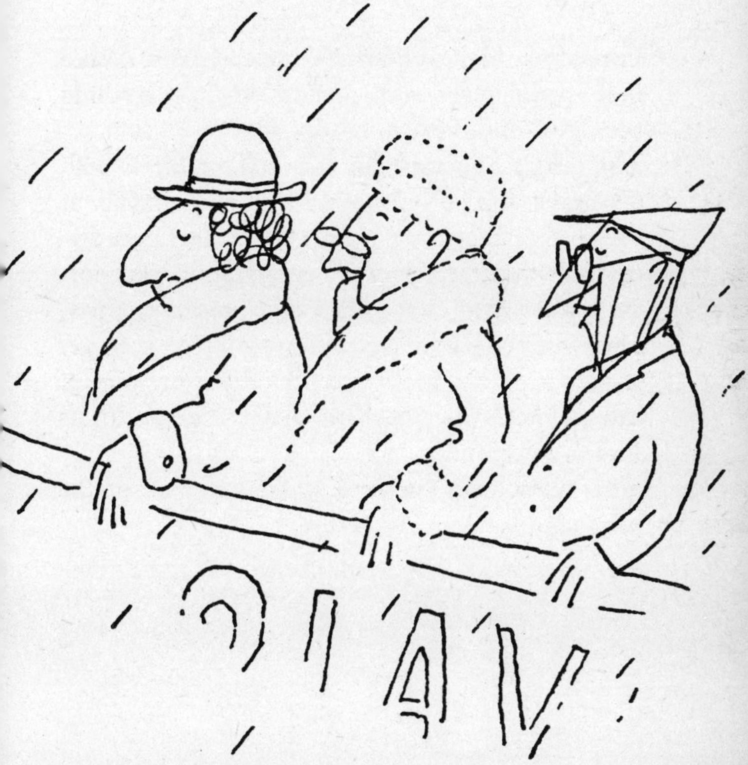

42
Professor Baba's Last Request
* * *

Professor Baba lies dying. Round his *futon* squat his wife and three sons. The professor wants his property to be divided equally among these four survivors, but realizes that any division he makes will probably not correspond to their respective estimates of the value of the shares. In his final moment of lucidity he devises a method according to which each of the four survivors will receive a share that he (or she) considers to be at least as valuable as those accruing to the other three. He explains the method to his grateful and admiring family. What is it?

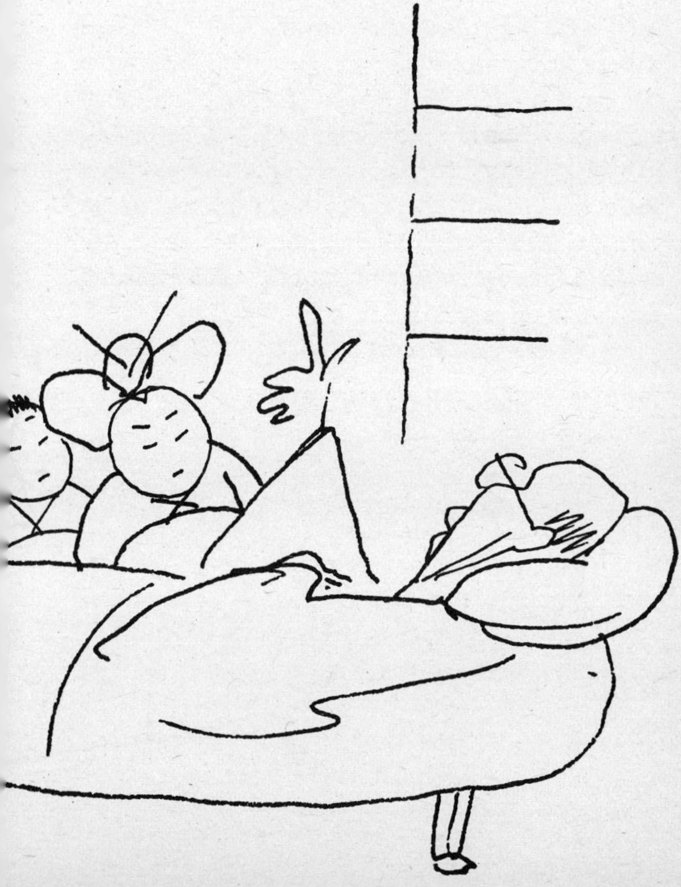

43
The Canny Landlord
*

Ten weary, footsore travellers,
All in a woeful plight,
Sought shelter at a wayside inn
One dark and stormy night.

'Nine rooms, no more,' the landlord said,
'Have I to offer you.
To each of eight a single bed,
But the ninth must serve for two.'

A din arose. The troubled host
Could only scratch his head,
For of those tired men no two
Would occupy one bed.

The puzzled host was soon at ease—
He was a clever man—
And so to please his guests devised
This most ingenious plan.

In a room marked A two men were placed,
The third was lodged in B,
The fourth to C was then assigned,
The fifth retired to D.

In E the sixth he tucked away,
In F the seventh man,
The eighth and ninth in G and H,
And then to A he ran,

Wherein the host, as I have said,
Had laid two travellers by;
Then taking one—the tenth and last—
He lodged him safe in I.

Nine single rooms—a room for each—
Were made to serve for ten;
And this it is that puzzles me
And many wiser men.

What is the fallacy?

(*From a 19th-century English magazine, quoted by Martin Gardner*)

44
Charles XII's Interrupted Game
* * *

When Charles XII of Sweden was besieged by the Turkish army in Bender, he played a game of chess that reached the following position:

The King (White) had announced mate in three moves when a Turkish bullet shattered his Knight. After a moment's examination Charles XII announced that even without the Knight he could give mate in four moves. Thereupon another bullet demolished his pawn at KR2. 'I can still mate you,'

said the king, 'but now it will take five moves.'
What were the three moves, the four moves and
the five moves?

(*Invented by the great American puzzlist, Sam Loyd*)

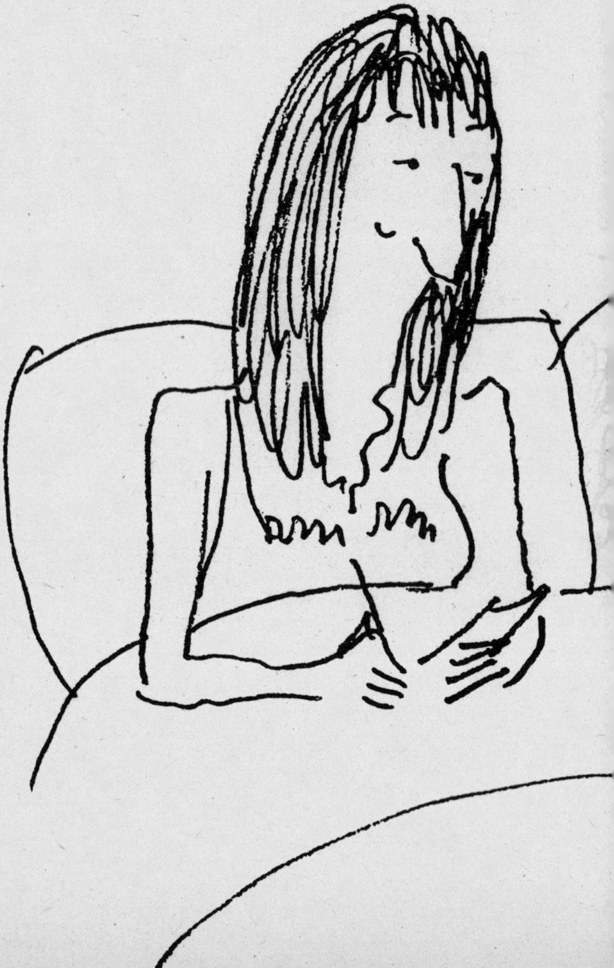

45
Prunella and her Lover
*

Prunella lives with Boris, whom she adores. During the first half of 1972 they make love 'two days on and one day off'. At the end of the year Prunella realizes that in 1972 Boris has made love to her on an average of exactly seven times in three weeks. How many times did they make love during the second half of the year?

46
Professor Baba's Little Game
* * *

Professor Baba was in a playful mood as he boarded the train for his summer (1972) holidays in Atami Hot Springs. Noticing one of his assistant lecturers, a bright young man called Honda, he said, 'Think of any card that is not a jack, queen, or king. Now, if it is black, add ten to the number of the card; if it is red, do not change your number. Then multiply by ten. Add the size of your shoes. Add two hundred if your suit is hearts or clubs. If you have visited a bar or beer-hall this week, add five hundred. Now multiply by two and add thirty-nine, and then multiply by fifty. If you have had a birthday since the beginning of this year, add twenty-two; if not, add twenty-one. If you had a bath today, add thirty. Subtract the year in which you were born. If you prefer whisky to *sake*, subtract ninety thousand. Now, Mr Honda, what is your number?' 'Minus 50,036,' replied the Assistant.

Thereupon Professor Baba was able to tell: (i) whether or not Honda preferred whisky, (ii) whether he had had a bath that day, (iii) his age, (iv) whether or not he had been to a bar or a beer-hall

[68]

that week, (v) the number and suit of his card, (vi) his size in shoes.
What are (i) to (vi)?

Supplementary: What would Professor Baba have learnt about his assistant if the reply had been 78,730?

47
Hippies
* *

What conclusion can be drawn from these 8 premises:
(a) Everyone who works in the I.B.M. Data Dump has shingles;

(b) all hippies are unhappy;
(c) no one whose mother is, or has been, a shaman suffers simultaneously from shingles and mixed dominance;
(d) Christoph L. Biggleswade works in the I.B.M. Data Dump;
(e) all hippies are fluent in Kpelle and Fang;
(f) Christoph L. Biggleswade is a hippy;
(g) everyone fluent in Kpelle and Fang is a candidate for the Doctor's degree, or else his mother is, or has been, a shaman;
(h) no one who is unhappy can be a candidate for the Ph.D.

(Devised by Professor H. Webb)

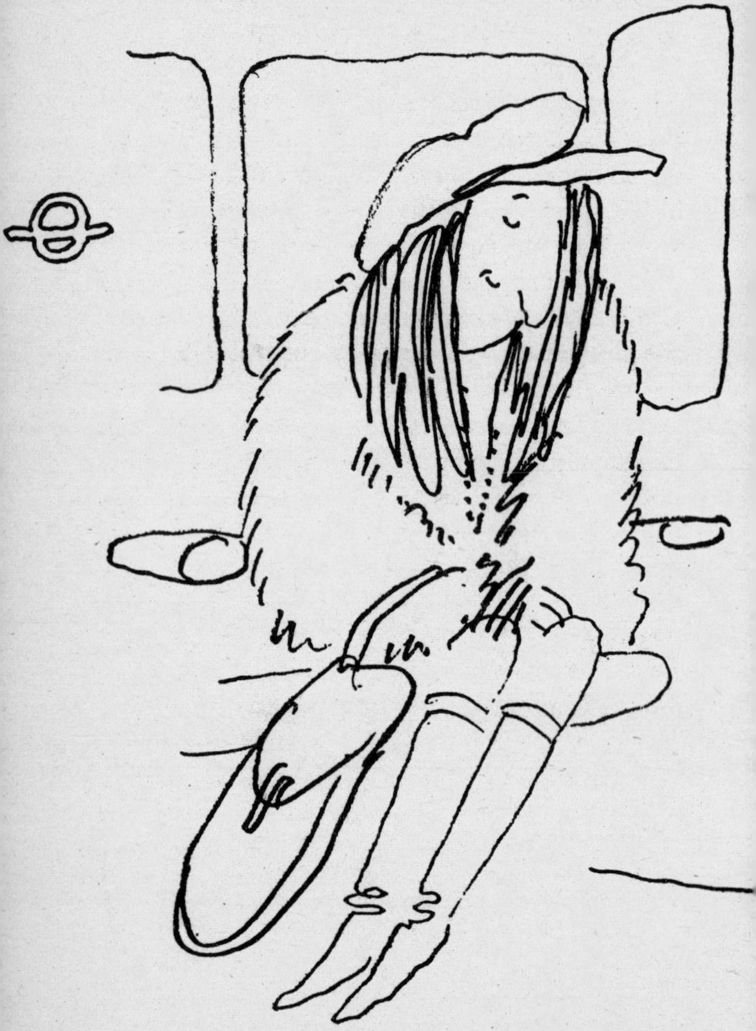

48
Belinda's Lovers

*

Belinda has two lovers, Cecil and Cedric, and she travels frequently on the underground to visit them in their respective flats. The train that takes her towards Cecil leaves from the opposite side of the platform from the one that takes her towards Cedric. Since Belinda enjoys the two men equally, and since they are both always available for her in the afternoons and do not require any advance notice of her visits, she simply takes the first train that happens to come along, regardless of whether it will take her to Cecil or to Cedric. She assumes that in the long run this will let her spend equal time with each of her lovers. In fact, however, she finds that on an average she is visiting Cedric four times out of five. Why?

(Based on an idea by Martin Gardner)

49
Digits
*

What is the largest number that can be written with three digits?

50
Mrs Tabako's Balls
* *

Mrs Tabako keeps her three pairs of magnetic balls in three Ming jars. Three of the balls are coloured gold and three silver, and two are kept in each jar, labelled GG (two gold balls), SS (two silver balls), and GS (one ball of each colour). One day Mr Tabako playfully changes his wife's labels so that all three jars are incorrectly labelled. If Mrs Tabako realizes that the labels are now all wrong, how many balls must she extract in order to determine the precise content of each jar?

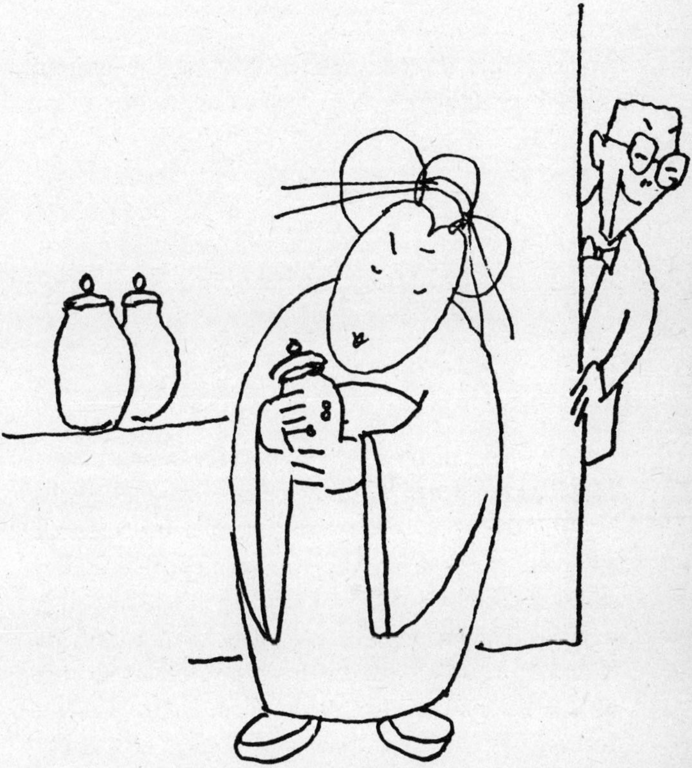

51
American Scholars

*

'By Jove!' said old Professor Carruthers, looking at a history book recently published by an American university press. 'These trans-Atlantic scholar chaps make some funny mistakes in their dates. Here are three mistakes on a single page—8th March instead of 3rd August, 7th April instead of 4th July, and 9th August instead of 8th September, an average of about ninety days earlier in each case than it should be.'

In fact the American scholar's book was entirely accurate. What 'discrepancy' would Professor Carruther find if the book has a date corresponding to 8th August?

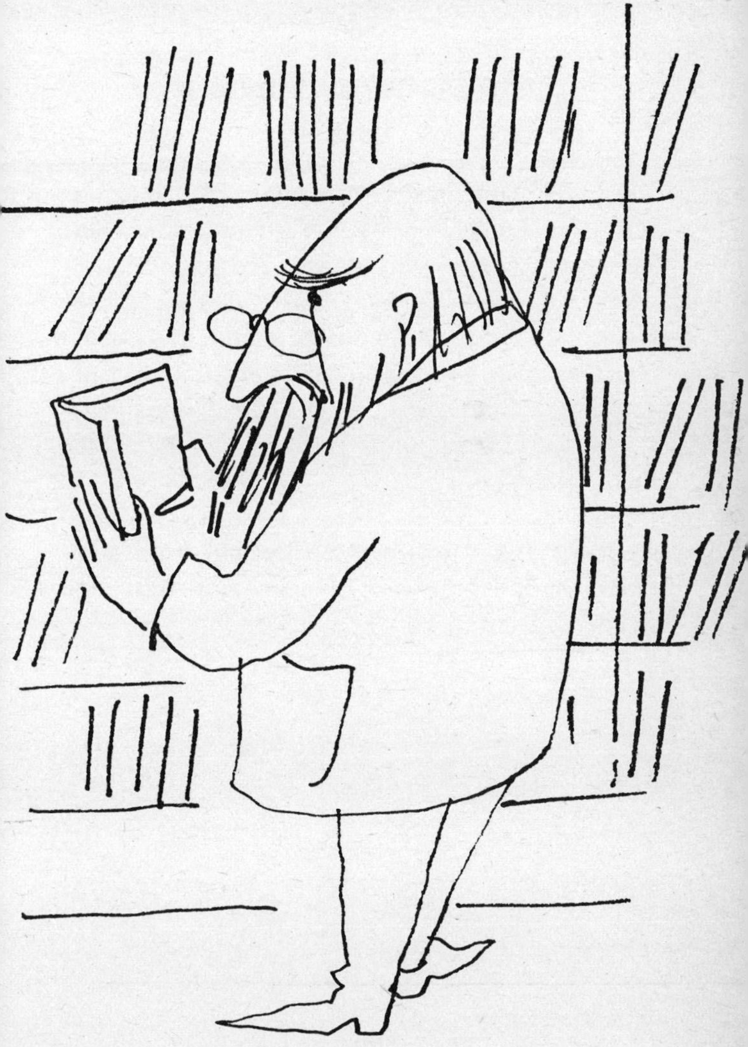

52
Lord Dunsany's Problem
**

White to play and mate in four moves.

53
Japanese Uncles
* *

Kazu no Ōji, a Crown Prince of Japan in the 5th century, was the uncle of Prince Asuka, and at the same time Prince Asuka was Kazu no Ōji's uncle. Would such a relationship be possible without violating the Christian laws of marriage?

54
Tempus Fugit
* *

Carefully examine the following passage and then explain the precise meaning of the first sentence (if possible by translating it into French): TIME FLIES. I CAN'T. THEY MOVE TOO FAST.

(*This was given as part of a test for U.N. translators*)

55
Ship of Fools
* *

Fifteen passengers have been invited to dine at the Captain's Table. The Captain is given the following alphabetical list, which shows their ages and occupations.

Peter Abbot, young American architect (31)

Paul Behrer, Swiss photographer (38)

Hugo Furst, psychiatrist (disciple of Sigmund Freud) (75)

Otto Jennarian, dealer in Oriental rugs (53)

Sonny Lamatina, restaurateur from New York (51)

Moira Less, choreographer from London (43)

Clara Nette, companion to Anne Schluss (45)

Peter Rast, sports master at boys' preparatory school (31)

Tommy Rast, golf professional, brother of Peter Rast (26)

D. S. E. Ray, Bombay-based independent film producer (49)

Anne Schluss, widow of Heinrich Schluss (the munitions magnate) (73)

René Sens, French interior decorator (48)

Justin Thaïm, Anglo-Egyptian poet (42)

R. N. G'u Than, diplomat in Burmese Mission to the United Nations (43)
Mah Tze-pan, Taiwanese screw manufacturer (50)

Who is the odd man out?

(*Prepared in co-operation with Mr and Mrs Lewis of Hancock, New Hampshire*)

56
Foul Play

*

'I suspect foul play,' muttered Detective Inspector Grimmins as he examined the room. The dead man lay slumped over his desk, blood trickling from the wound in his forehead. On the floor to the right of the desk was a small German revolver. On the left of the desk Grimmins noticed a piece of strong silk cord, which suggested a connexion with the bright red line round the dead man's neck. The gramophone was still playing the final act of Wagner's Götterdämmerung, and there was an unmistakable smell of opium in the room. The dead man was entirely naked except for a pair of black net stockings and an emerald necklace.
'Excuse me, sir,' said Police Constable Higgins. 'I've found what appears to be a suicide note. It says, "My last Will and Testament can be found between pages 255 and 256 of volume 2 of the Wagner biography on top of the bookshelf behind my desk."'
'Oh no, it can't, 'said Detective Inspector Grimmins.
Why?

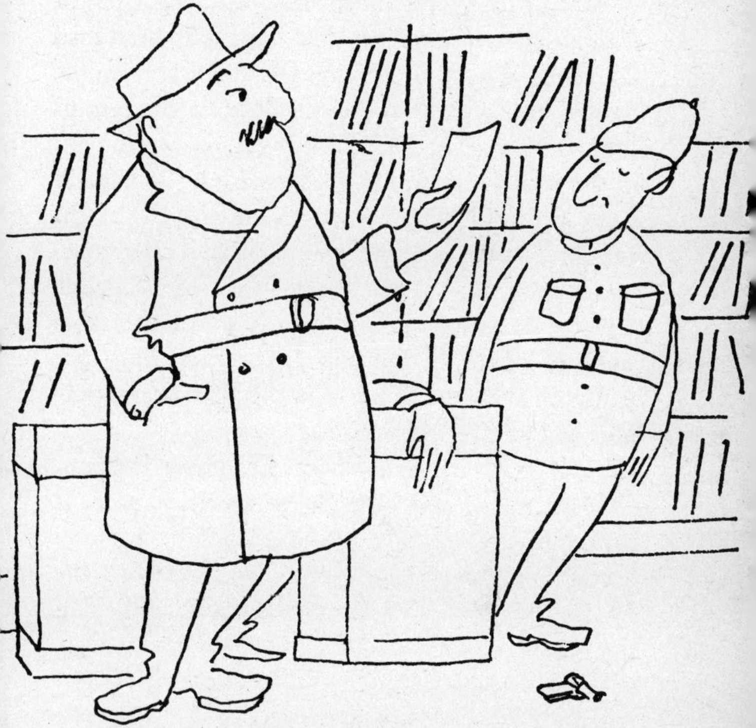

SOLUTIONS

SOLUTIONS

1

He juggles them as he runs across.

2

I ... it ... tie ... rite ... inter ... retain ... certain ... reaction ... cremation ... importance.

3

He plants three of the trees at the corners of an equilateral triangle and then builds a mound in the centre of the triangle where he plants the fourth tree.

4

Chorax thinks, 'If the judge says I must pay, I shall have lost my first case and, according to our private agreement, I shall be absolved from my obligation; if he says I need not pay, I am legally clear.'
Phaedo thinks, 'If the judge says Chorax must pay, he will be legally obliged to do so; if the judge excuses

him from paying, Chorax will have won his first case and our agreement will oblige him to pay.'

Both men are wrong since they are shifting their criteria. According to the legal criterion, the judge's public decision is conclusive; according to the private moral criterion, it is the terms of the agreement that count. Either criterion must be chosen, but it must be used consistently. One cannot get it both ways. If, for example, one chooses to be guided by the legal criterion (i.e. by the judge's decision), this criterion must supersede all others and the terms of the private agreement become irrelevant.

5

Yes, because 1 new penny = 2·4 old pennies and 24 old pennies = 2 shillings (= 10 new pence).
With 50 or more new pence the result of doubling is three digits; with less than five, one digit.

6

Vile ... evil ... veil ... Levi ... live.

7

(a) Nightmare, (b) Cowlick.

8

4 ounces $\left(2+\dfrac{x}{2} = x \text{ and } 4+x = 2x\right)$.

9

They had no navels.

10

Luster ... rulest ... Ulster ... lurest ... luter's ... lustre ... rustle ... sutler ... result.

11

One hopes that the survivors would be allowed to remain above ground.

12

(*a*) One in three (*OE, EO, OO*).
(*b*) One in two (*OE, EE*).

13

A ... an ... and ... dean ... Arden ... snared ... wardens ... answered ... wanderer's ... underwear's.

14

He places his hand against the right (or left) wall and keeps it there as he walks. By this method he is eventually bound to reach the exit, even though his route may be very circuitous.

15

134,689. As usual in puzzles of this kind, it is best to start with small, easy numbers. The series of square numbers, beginning with the square of 1, is 1 ... 4 ... 9 ... 16 ... 25 ... 36. The differences between these numbers are 3, 5, 7, 9, 11. In other words, the difference between any square number and the next one in the series is always two greater than the difference between it and the preceeding one in the series. Since the difference between the numbers in this puzzle is 731, the next square number in the series must be 133,956 + 733 = 134,689.

16

A few seconds after 9.49 (to be absolutely precise, it is forty-nine and one eleventh of a minute after nine o'clock). A formula can be rapidly produced by observing that the minute hand moves 60 minutes in the time that the hour hand requires in order to move 5 minutes

$$x = \frac{x+540}{12}.$$

17

'*I am going to be garrotted.*'

18

99. If 'some' were large and 'some' small, it is possible that there may have been 98 large tablets and 2 small ones. It is also possible that the first 98 pills he extracted were all large; in that case the 99th pill was bound to be small and he would then know that the others were all large. (On the other hand, if the first two pills happened to be of different sizes, he would immediately know which was large.)

19

The squeamish surgeon is Mrs McKeetch, Bruce's mother. (Anyone who fails to answer this question has prima facie *grounds for suspecting that he may suffer from 'male chauvinism'.)*

20

A ... at ... eat ... tear ... irate ... retina ... reliant ... Oriental ... lion-tamer ... trampoline

21

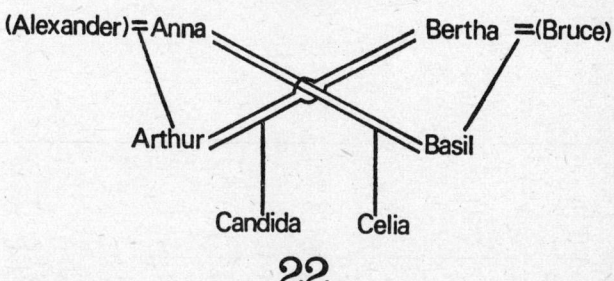

```
(Alexander)=Anna          Bertha=(Bruce)
         \   /            
          \ /
           X
          / \
       Arthur  Basil
       Candida  Celia
```

22

897 A.D. $(x-845 = 2(x-871)$
$x-845 = 2x-1742)$.

23

(a) *dove ... hove ... have ... hare ... hark ... hawk.*

(b) *money ... honey ... honed ... toned ... towed ... tower ... power.*

(c) *water ... mater ... mates ... males ... moles ... boles ... bolts ... boots ... booty ... boozy ... booze.*

(d) *blood ... blond ... blend ... bleed ... bleep ... sleep ... sweep ... sweet ... sweat ... sweet ... sheet ... sheer ... shier ... shies ... shims ... shams ... seams ... sears ... tears.*

(*Solutions to* (b), (c), *and* (d) *improved by Dr H. W. Hazard*)

24

1. Q×P ch. (!)   K×Q
2. N×B dbl. ch.   K–R3 (if K–R, N–N6 mate)
3. KN–N4 ch.   K–N4
4. P–R4 ch.   K–B5
5. P–N3 ch.   K–B6
6. B–N2 ch.   K–N7
7. R–R2 ch.   K–N8
8. castles (mate).

White can also mate on his 8th move by simply moving his king, but then he deprives himself of the rare satisfaction of castling into a checkmate.

25

I HATE THEE STERILE ANAGRAM.

26

72 bees.

27

No, the Church in its wisdom does not allow the dead to marry.

28

The only prime factors into which 999,919 can be divided are 991 and 1,009. So each of the 991 soldiers killed 1,009 inhabitants—a veritable holocaust.

29

e.

30

Yes. However vast the expanse of sea, there has to be a point of intersection in the course of the journey, which follows a course like a reversed figure 4.

31

-ENT and -INE produce 12 words (bent, cent, dent, gent, hent, lent, pent, rent, sent, tent, vent, went and bine, dine, fine, kine, line, mine, nine, pine, sine, tine, vine, wine), -ILL gives 13 words (bill, dill, fill, gill, hill, kill, mill, nill, pill, rill, sill, till, will) and so does James Michie's -AIL (bail, fail, hail, jail, kail, mail, nail, pail, rail, sail, tail, vail, wail).

32

The eldest child was born in 1961; the triplets were born ten years later (ages: 11-1-1-1).

33

I . . . in . . . nil . . . Nile . . . lines . . . listen . . . salient . . . entrails . . . intervals . . . starveling . . . everlasting . . . never-staling

34

'Draw' is the only one without a participle in -ught, rhyming with 'taut'.

35

'The reasoning' (explains *The New York Times*) *'is that the authorities would think the hijacker was going to ask the stewardess or a member of the crew to parachute with him, and thus would be sure to provide parachutes that opened.'*

36

Since it makes no difference whether the thermometer is Fahrenheit or Centigrade, the temperature must be exactly 40 degrees below zero.

$$\frac{(x-32) \times 5}{9} = x$$
$$5x - 160 = 9x$$
$$x = -40.$$

37

(a) *Watanabe cannot be the Assistant Captain;*
(b) *Mr Abe lives in Tokyo;*
(c) *the wrestler lives in Kamakura; he cannot be Mr Abe (who lives in Tokyo), nor can he be Mr Tanabe (who is a cripple), so he must be Mr Watanabe;*
(d) *we now know that Messrs Watanabe and Abe live in Kamakura and Tokyo respectively; therefore Mr Tanabe must live in Yokohama;*
(e) *we can now tell that the Captain is Tanabe;*
(f) *since the Assistant Captain is neither Watanabe nor Tanabe, he must be Abe;*

(g) this means that Abe cannot be the Chief Stewardess; and, since neither Tanabe nor Abe holds that position, it must be Miss (or Mrs) Watanabe.

Supplementary: *Mr Abe is dead wrong. The fact that he carries a bomb in no way affects the chances that other passengers may also be doing so. The one definite effect of his carrying his own bomb is that it may go off by mistake.*

38

'Jews vend big film; hock quartz pyx' (28 letters, James Michie, Esq.)
'Five bawds mock quartz-glyph jinx' (28 letters, Dr H. W. Hazard).
Longer but more appealing is James Michie's 'Quick, fox, and jump this blowzy grove' (30 letters).

39

Four. 'Twice four and twenty' can mean either 48 or 28. Since 48 is not divisible by 7, there were obviously 28 blackbirds, and Jill must have shot 4. These 4 remained and the other 24 were naturally frightened by the blast and flew away.

40

However many letters you start with, you get exactly the same number of combinations in the two cases. In the case of the 25-letter combinations the missing 26th letter can be added to each of the possible combinations.

41

Four. The human brain usually concentrates on the more interesting and challenging aspects of a question, even if they may not be the most important ones. Most solvers are likely to think about the numbers of passengers (50-150-100-90-100) rather than about the number of stops.

42

If they can agree to divide into 2 'teams' of two, one team would divide the property in half, and the other team would choose a half; then one member of each team would subdivide his team's half, and the other would choose his quarter, so all would be satisfied. If they cannot agree sufficiently, let W = wife and X, Y, and Z, the sons. W divides the property in quarters and each son indicates his first choice. If all chose differently (A, B, C), W gets D and all are satisfied. If X and Y choose A, and Z chooses B, give it to him and tell X and Y to indicate their second choices. If both choose C, give D to W and tell X and Y to divide A and C in the usual way. If X chooses C and Y chooses D, tell each to subdivide his choice and let W choose half of each (C and D), with the balance going to X and Y, who divide A in the usual way. This is a 9/16 chance, and all differing is 6/16, leaving all the same 1/16, in which case they do it over, with X instead of W dividing. He will make A smaller, so W will not want it, and thus eventually a choice will be made that satisfies everyone. (Solution by Dr H. W. Hazard)

43

The fallacy is in line 3 of the penultimate stanza. The two men lodged in A were the first and the second; the tenth was still unlodged.

44

Three moves:
   1. R×P   B×R
   2. N–B3   black must move his bishop
   3. P–N4 mate
if 1.   B×N
   2. R–R3 ch.   B–R5
   3. P–N4 mate

Four moves:
   1. P×P   B–K6
   2. R–N4   B–N4
   3. R–R4 ch.   B×R
   4. P–N4 mate

Five moves:
   1. R–QN7   B–K6
   2. R–N   B–N4
   3. R–R ch.   B–R5
   4. R–R2   P×R
   5. P–N4 mate
if 1. . . .   B–N8
   2. R–N   B–R7
   3. R–K   K–R5
   4. R–N6   any move
   5. R–K4 mate

45

Not a single time. Since the average for the year was 1/3 and the average for the first half of the year 2/3, the average for the second half must be 0.

46

(i) prefers whisky; (ii) had a bath today, (iii) 34 (born in spring 1938); (iv-v) 9 clubs; no bar; (vi) size 9.
Supplementary: (i) prefers sake; (ii) no bath; (iii) 30 (born in autumn 1941); (iv-v) 8 hearts; bar; (vi) size 7.
The sequences of numbers are:
9 ... 19 ... 190 ... 199 ... 399 ... 798 ... 837 ... 8370 ... 41850 ... 41872 ... 41902 ... 39964 ... minus 50036 and (supplementary) 8 ... 80 ... 87 ... 287 ... 787 ... 1574 ... 1613 ... 16130 ... 80650 ... 80671 ... 80671 ... 78730.

Analysis of final numbers;
  (i) prefers whisky: negative number (add 90,000)
    prefers sake: positive number (add nothing)

[102]

(ii) *had a bath today: last two digits obviously 30 years higher than age, so subtract 30 to find the age.*

(iii) *last two digits (e.g. $39 \times 50 = 1950$*
$+ 21 =$ last birthday in 1971
$+ 22 =$ last birthday in 1972)

	d.	s.	h.	c.
(iv–v) *no bar or beer-hall*	0	1	2	3
bar or beer-hall	5	6	7	8

Here the hierarchy of the 1st digit goes from diamonds without bar ($= 0$) to clubs with bar ($= 1 + 2 + 5 = 8$)

(vi) *middle figure of final digit.*

The multiplication steps, being aimed at securing new digits at the right of the existing number, involve multiplication by 10 or a power of 10. The second step moves the decimal point one place to the right, the 6th and 8th steps combine to move it two places to the right $\left(\dfrac{100}{50} \times 50\right)$.

47

Christoph L. Biggleswade does not suffer from mixed dominance. (Premises b, f, and h combine to tell us that Biggleswade is not a Ph.D. candidate; from premises a and d we know that he has shingles, and from e and f that he is fluent in Kpelle and Fang. If we take g into account, we therefore know that his mother is, or has been, a shaman; this is combined with c to produce the final conclusion.)

48

The trains leave at five-minute intervals, and the one that goes in Cedric's direction always arrives a minute before the other one. Therefore the Cecil-bound train will arrive first only if Belinda appears on the platform during the one-minute interval between the two trains; on an average this will happen only once in five times. (N.B. 5–1 in this solution could of course be 10–2, 15–3, etc.)

49

$9^{(9^9)}$ (i.e. 9 to the power of 9^9). This is a rather large number (cf. 10 to the power of 10^{10} is 1 followed by ten thousand million zeroes).

50

Only one ball. She takes it from the jar labelled GS. If it is gold, she knows that the other ball in the jar must also be gold. The balls in the GG jar must therefore both be silver, and those in the SS jar are gold and silver. Similar reasoning applies if the ball she draws from the GS jar is silver.

51

No discrepancy at all since the day and the number of the month are identical. Obviously the book gave the dates in numerals arranged in the usual American order (3/10 for 10th March, etc.), but Carruthers read them in the English order (so that for him 3/10 would represent 3rd October).

52

(a) Black's king and queen are not on their original squares;

(b) they must therefore have moved;

(c) this means that some black pawn must have moved;

(d) but all the pawns appear to be on their 2nd rank, and pawns cannot move backwards;

(e) so the black pawns reached their present positions from the other side of the board and are now in fact on their 7th rank.

A checkmate for white is therefore quite easy; in the following solution the squares are identified as they appear to be in the diagram, though actually what appears to be white's B1 is his B8, black's K3 is his K6, etc.:

1. KN–K2	N–QR3
2. N–B4	any move
3. N–K6 checkmate	
if 1. . . .	N–QB3
2. N–B4	N–QR3
3. R × N	any move
4. N–K6 checkmate.	

[106]

53

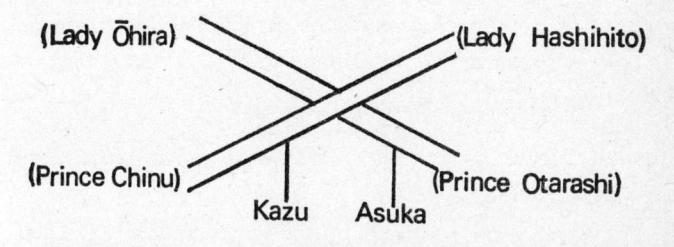

```
(Lady Ōhira)              (Lady Hashihito)
           \            /
            \          /
             \        /
              \      /
               \    /
                \  /
                 \/
                 /\
                /  \
               /    \
              /      \
(Prince Chinu)        (Prince Otarashi)
            Kazu   Asuka
```

Prince Kazu is the half-brother of Prince Asuka's father, and at the same time Prince Asuka is the half-brother of Prince Kazu's father. So they are each other's uncles. (Also, of course, they are each other's nephews.) For the Christian laws of marriage to be respected both Lady Ōhira and Lady Hashihito must have been widowed when they married Prince Otarashi and Prince Chinu respectively.

54

The clue is the unexpected word 'they', which must refer to a plural antecedent. This antecedent can only be 'flies' (the plural of the insect). 'Time' must therefore be the imperative of the verb 'to time' (of which the French translation would be chronometrez*). The first sentence is an order to time (i.e. to note the speed of) a group of flies.*

[107]

55

Tommy Rast. His is the only name on the list that is not susceptible to the following kind of alteration: Peter Rabbit, Pall-bearer, You Go First, Octogenarian, Sonnez les matines, More or Less, Clarinet, Paederast, Dies Irae, Anschluss, Renaissance, Just in Time, Orang-utan, Marzipan.

56

The answer can be found by examing the first book you pick up. All self-respecting printers insist that even-numbered pages must be on the left and odd-numbered pages on the right.

IVAN MORRIS has written widely on modern and ancient Japan and has translated numerous works from both classical and contemporary Japanese literature. In 1965 he received the Duff Cooper Award for his book *The World of the Shining Prince*. In 1968 his translation of *The Pillow-Book of Sei Shonagon* won exceptionally high praise on both sides of the Atlantic. More recently he edited *Madly Singing in the Mountains*, an appreciation and anthology of Arthur Waley. At present he is Professor of Japanese at Columbia University in New York.